It's Hard to be Good

K.J. HALES

ILLUSTRATED BY **SERENE WYATT**

opendoor
press inc.

Life's Little Lessons by

Lesson #1 - It's Hard to be Good

First Edition
Text copyright © 2015 by K.J. Hales (www.kjhales-author.com)
Illustrations copyright © 2015 by Serene Wyatt (www.serenewyatt.com)
Book Design by Michael Penman/PenmanWorks (www. PenmanWorks.com)
Book Production and Development with AJ & Associates, LLC (www.ajandassociates.com)
Go Boom! font created by Miguel Rios

ISBN #978-1-942264-02-6

Publisher's Cataloging-In-Publication Data

Hales, K. J.
  It's hard to be good / K.J. Hales ; illustrated by Serene Wyatt. -- First edition.
   pages : color illustrations ; cm. -- (Life's little lessons by Ellie the Weinerdog ; lesson #1)
  Summary: Ellie the Weinerdog faces temptation and has to make a choice between right and wrong.
  ISBN: 978-1-942264-02-6
  1. Right and wrong--Juvenile fiction. 2. Conduct of life--Juvenile fiction. 3. Dachshunds--Juvenile fiction. 4. Right and wrong--Fiction. 5. Conduct of life--Fiction. 6. Dachshunds--Fiction. 7. Stories in rhyme. I. Wyatt, Serene. II. Title.
PZ7.1.H35 I87 2015
[E]   2015912838

Printed in the USA

visit us at
opendoor-press.com/ellie-the-wienerdog

opendoor
press inc.

It's hard to be good.

It's hard to be good,

when I get a whiff.

One smell in the air
and I must go see

what yummy treats might be waiting for me.

Today I'm in luck,
for what do I see?

A freshly made
sandwich

CALLING

to me.

and I curl at their feet.

sit

stay

read

www.elliethewienerdog.com

opendoor press inc.